HELGA MAKES A NAME FOR HERSELF

by Megan Maynor   Illustrated by Eda Kaban

CLARION BOOKS | Houghton Mifflin Harcourt | Boston   New York

For my warriors—clear-eyed, clever, and strong—
Chloe, Emmett, and Willa. —M.M.

To all the girls who were told they can't,
but did it anyway! —E.K.

Clarion Books, 3 Park Avenue, New York, New York 10016

Text copyright © 2020 by Megan Maynor
Illustrations copyright © 2020 by Eda Kaban

Clarion Books is an imprint of
Houghton Mifflin Harcourt Publishing Company.

hmhbooks.com

The illustrations in this book were done digitally.
The text was set in Amanda Std.
Book design by Sharismar Rodriguez

Library of Congress Cataloging-in-Publication Data is available.
Names: Maynor, Megan, author. | Kaban, Eda, illustrator.
Title: Helga makes a name for herself / by Megan Maynor ;
    illustrated by Eda Kaban.
Description: New York : Clarion Books, [2020] | Audience: Ages 4 to 7.
Audience: Grades K–1. | Summary: A small but fierce Viking girl,
    along with her wolverine sidekick, is determined to become a warrior,
    just like her hero Ingrid the Axe.
Identifiers: LCCN 2019036636 | ISBN 9781328957832 (hardcover)
Subjects: CYAC: Determination (Personality trait)—Fiction. | Sex
    role—Fiction. | Vikings—Fiction.
Classification: LCC PZ7.1.M388 He 2020 | DDC [E]—dc23
LC record available at https://lccn.loc.gov/2019036636

Manufactured in China
SCP 10 9 8 7 6 5 4 3 2 1
4500800866

YOUNG HELGA loved to hear the sagas of her favorite Viking warrior.

She begged for them at bedtime,

and fish-pickling time,

and during her monthly bath.

After Helga made herself a helmet—and one for her pet wolverine—
she asked her mother, "What do you think my warrior name will be?"

Helga built herself a shield—and one for Wolvie—and asked her father, "What do you think my warrior name will be?"

Helga's father laughed.

Warriors do not come from small mountain villages like ours.

Helga forged herself a sword—and one for Wolvie—and asked her neighbor Sven Longbeard, "What do you think my warrior name will be?"

"Helga!" called her mother. "Time to do yer chores!"

Helga raced up steep hills to graze the sheep—
as though enemies were in pursuit.

She chopped wood, imagining she
was breaking open a treasure chest.

And when her work was done, Helga and Wolvie reenacted the great battles of Ingrid the Axe—making them even greater.

One Thor's Day, word reached Helga's farm that Ingrid the Axe was looking for new warriors—and her ship would be arriving soon.

Faster than Valkyries fly, Helga and Wolvie donned their full battle gear.

"Helga," said her father,
"that contest is not for you."

"Helga," said her mother,
"remember who you are."

"Yah," said Helga.

'AM A WARRIORRR!

WHERE'S THE WILD BOAR?

In the port city, Helga and Wolvie saw more young Vikings than they'd seen in their entire lives—along with real helmets, painted shields, and shiny swords.

The other Vikings saw Helga and Wolvie too.

A horn sounded. *Ruh-Roooo!*
A giant voice boomed, "Gather 'round!"
Helga gasped. "Ingrid the Axe."
Wolvie fainted.

"I am looking for swift, mighty, clever warriors," said Ingrid. "Prove yourself and join my crew!"

"YAH!" the young Vikings cheered.

"First, a race!" said Ingrid.
Helga took her place at
the starting line.
   "Ready . . . and . . . go!"

After years of running up the mountainside, Helga was fast,

but when her homemade helmet slipped, Olaf pulled ahead.

"YOU!" Ingrid pointed her giant hand at Olaf. "OLAF . . . THE SWIFT! JOIN ME!"

"Next! Battle Axe Bullseye!"
Helga had swung an axe
plenty of times. How different
could it be to throw one?

A bit different, it turns out.
Sigrid threw a bull's-eye.
"YOU!" Ingrid pointed her giant hand at Sigrid.
"SIGRID . . . THE SURE SHOT, JOIN ME!"

"Last, Sword Fighting!"
Helga squared off against Magnus.
The other Vikings laughed. "This should be quick."
Hisss! Helga showed her teeth. Magnus jumped back.

They circled each other.

Helga got low and prowled in close. She tweaked Magnus's nose.

HEY!

Helga tapped Magnus's shoulder,
then spun around him.
Magnus turned and tripped.

Helga pounced on
her opponent
and howled,

AROOOO!

"What . . . happened?"
asked Magnus.

"YOU!" Ingrid pointed her giant hand at Helga. "You fight like a . . . wolverine."

Wolvie stood tall.

Ingrid continued, "HELGA—"

Helga's parents came charging down the hill.

"She won't bother you anymore,"
said Helga's mother.

"We'll take her home,"
said Helga's father.

"AHEM," said Ingrid,
"I was about to say, HELGA . . .
THE HOWLER! JOIN ME!"

"Our Helga?" asked her mother.
"Is that . . . a warrior's name?" asked her father.

Helga stood before her stunned parents. "I am a farmersdotter. I am from a small mountain village. And I AM A WARRIOR!"

Helga and Wolvie howled together.

AROOOO!

AROOOO!

Helga the Howler went on to sail
the whole flat earth—first with Ingrid the Axe.

Later, on her own ship.

And finally, as commander of her own
fleet of ships, Wolvie ever at her side.

In fact, to this day, young Vikings beg to hear the sagas of Helga.
During their nightly baths,
at pickle-pickling time,
and at bedtime.

"Tell me the one about
how she became . . .
HELGA THE HOWLER!"

AROOOO!

AUTHOR'S NOTE

This story is imagined. But Vikings were real.

Vikings lived hundreds of years ago, 1050–750 BCE, in what we now call Denmark, Norway, and Sweden.

Viking ships were revolutionary, able to navigate both the open sea and shallow waters. This allowed Vikings to expand to England, Scotland, Wales, Ireland, Iceland, Greenland, Estonia, France—and beyond. Vikings raided, traded, and sometimes settled, throughout Europe and Central Asia. Some traveled as far as North America and Jerusalem.

The most popular image of a Viking is that of a warrior, but most Vikings were farmers.

Vikings are also usually shown in horned helmets, as Helga and some of the other Vikings are in this book, but this look was actually made popular by a German costume designer producing an opera in the 1870s.

Real Viking warriors likely wore a simpler iron helmet (no horns), a leather helmet, or no helmet at all.

Shield maidens (bands of warrior women) are featured in sagas, poems, and Viking lore, but for a long time there was no evidence of real female Viking warriors. However, in 2017, DNA analysis of bones from a Viking burial site in Birka, Sweden, revealed the exalted warrior within—buried with a sword, an axe, a knife, two lances, two shields, and twenty-five arrows—was a woman.

Were there other warrior women like her? We don't know for sure—yet. Exciting new clues about Vikings are being discovered and studied to this day.

So, the saga continues . . .

P.S. Wolverines do not actually make good pets.

FOR FURTHER READING

BOOKS FOR CHILDREN

Everything Vikings by Nadia Higgins, published by National Geographic Society, 2015
Vikings by Therese Shea, published by Britannica Educational Publishing, 2017
Vikings by Philip Steele, published by DK Publishing, 2018

BOOKS FOR TEENS AND ADULTS

The Age of the Vikings by Anders Winroth, published by Princeton University Press, 2014

Viking Age: Everyday Life During the Extraordinary Era of the Norsemen by Kirsten Wolf, published by Sterling, 2004

WEBSITES

An overview of Vikings and Viking life for kids:
https://www.dkfindout.com/us/history/vikings/

Fun facts and an animated video about Vikings:
https://www.natgeokids.com/uk/discover/history/general-history/10-facts-about-the-vikings/

The Viking Phenomenon research project at Uppsala University,
featuring research from archeologists working today:
www.arkeologi.uu.se/Research/Projects/viking-phenomenon/

Academic research paper discussing the female Viking warrior identified in 2017:
http://uu.diva-portal.org/smash/get/diva2:1294858/FULLTEXT01.pdf